I dedicate this book to my boys, Aaron and Justin. You never cease to amaze your mom and I. You both bring such joy to our lives. Thank you for being you.

"IF EVERYONE WAS PERFECT, NO ONE WOULD BE SPECIAL"

Written and published by: Ron Italiano
Illustrated by: Jessica Rogers
Creative Direction by: Nicole Mazur

GET ME 1
choppywowwow.com

There once was a little dog named Choppy.
Choppy was not your typical dog.
He was in training school to be a helper dog,
a special kind of dog that helps people.

2

Choppy lived at the Spotswood
Training School where he worked hard
every day, hoping that one day
he would find his special person.

At the Spotswood Training School there were all types of dogs. Smart dogs, strong dogs...

and big dogs.

Choppy always worked hard. But as the weeks went by, he still did not find his special person.

You see, every helper dog needs
a special person. Choppy knew that,
and so did all the other dogs.

Especially Regina.

She would tell Choppy, "No one will pick you. You are too small and your ears don't match. Look at me. I am perfect in every way, and you are not!"

Choppy's friend, Old Rex, would tell him, "Don't listen to Regina."

"You are kind, caring and unique. Remember Choppy, if everyone was perfect, no one would be special."

It was Saturday morning, the busiest day of the week. All of the dogs were ready to show off their skills. Choppy was excited. This could be the day he finds his special person.

As people came to visit the school, they were all greeted by the owner, Ms. Dewy. She introduced them to all of the dogs.

But as the day went along, Choppy did not get many visitors.

He watched while some of the dogs found homes.

Choppy was sad and thought he may never find his special person.

14

15

It was almost closing time. All of the visitors were gone, when a family walked in and asked Ms. Dewy if they were still open.

She said, "Yes, but we will be closing soon."

A Mom and Dad walked in with a little boy.

Mom said, "Come on AJ, don't be afraid. Let's look at all the bow wows."

Dad worried, "This is a bad idea."

Ms. Dewy said, "Hello young man, what is your name?" AJ did not answer.

AJ was not your typical boy. He did not talk much and moved his hands a lot. AJ did not look at the dogs and covered his ears, afraid that they would bark at him.

Mom, Dad, and AJ walked around the school visiting the dogs. Most of the time, AJ was hiding behind his mom.

She said, "AJ, look at all the bow wows!"

"Look at this cute little one!", Mom exclaimed as she walked up to Choppy.

Choppy laid on the ground and looked at AJ with his big eyes and his floppy ear.

AJ peeked out from behind his mom and smiled.

She said, "His name is Choppy, that's a cute name!"

Ms. Dewy approached the family and said, "Sorry, but we have to close now."

Mom replied, "OK, maybe we will come back another day."

Mom, Dad, and AJ walked back to the car.

Choppy was very sad. He told Old Rex,
"I liked him. I think he is my special person!"

Old Rex said, "I am sorry Choppy. I know
one day you will find someone very special,
just like you."

Back at the car, Dad was putting on AJ's seat belt. Suddenly, AJ looked his father in the eyes and said, "Choppy Wow Wow." Dad's eyes lit up.

Dad exclaimed, "Mom! Did you hear that?
AJ said Choppy Wow Wow! The dog!
The little dog inside! He said his name!"

Dad ran back to the school, yelling at the front gate. "Open Up, Open Up! We will take him! We want Choppy Wow Wow!"

Choppy heard Dad calling his name.
The whole family came back to the school.
AJ walked up to Choppy, smiled, pet him
on the head and said, "Choppy Wow Wow."
Choppy found his special person.

Dad said, "Come on Choppy Wow Wow, let's go home."

And so begins...
The Special Adventures of Choppy Wow Wow.

WHAT WORKS FOR US:

My wife and I try to expose our boys to different experiences and situations to see where their enjoyment and passion lies. Unlike typical children, our boys may not say, "I want to try this" or "I like doing that." So whether it is skiing, snorkeling, traveling, concerts, or playing different sports, just get out there. Every child is unique. Try new things, learn, and adjust accordingly.

ABOUT THE AUTHOR:

Ron Italiano is a first time author, born and raised in New Jersey. Over twenty years ago, Ron created the Choppy Wow Wow character to entertain his nieces with stories of kindness and positivity. Once he had children of his own, he continued to tell his stories but they took on a different meaning. Ron is the father of two boys with Autism. Ron and his wife would read nightly to their children and this is where he introduced his Choppy Wow Wow stories to them. As his boys struggled with communication, Ron turned the tables on his older son and asked him to tell a story. His son started his story with "There once was a dog named Choppy Wow Wow" and continued to tell him about his day, for the first time ever! His son would continue to develop his story telling skills and communicate through the eyes of Choppy Wow Wow. Ron wrote this book as the first in a series intended to promote inclusion, enjoyment of reading, and celebrating differences. It is his hope that these books will also help special needs parents navigate some of the parenting challenges that we all experience. He hopes you enjoy the book as much as he enjoyed writing it.

ABOUT THE ILLUSTRATOR:

Jessica Rogers is the niece of Ron Italiano, the author. She was born and raised in New Jersey and is a first-time illustrator. She pursued drawing as a hobby but after hearing the story of Choppy Wow Wow, she jumped at the opportunity to collaborate with her uncle on this book. She was excited about this series because of her close relationship with her two cousins, who are on the autism spectrum. Jessica is an occupational therapy graduate student with hopes to work with children with neurological, social, and behavioral disorders. Through her OT program, she has learned that incorporating different learning tactics, exposing children to various types of media, and finding time to encourage social interaction and mental stimulation can improve the health and wellbeing of these populations. Diverse representation on TV, media, and books also provides a sense of inclusivity among underrepresented or misrepresented populations. With that in mind, Jessica strived to create characters that would represent some members of the special needs community and their families. Jessica believes that simply reading this book for 10 minutes before bed can be the start of a rewarding journey for kids and families of all backgrounds and circumstances. She hopes that these unique characters can resonate with just one unique child.